Gwen and Jill join a rock 'n' roll band. Soon they discover that there's a special rock contest on TV for kids. All they have to do is come up with an original song. They play and try to write. During their work sessions they order pizza. When Jill's dog, Fletcher, begins to howl, he gives them the idea for a winning song, and they make him a member of the band.

Hundreds of kids show up for tryouts, but no one else has a dog, and Fletcher and the Gang make the finals. Then, one day at the dress rehearsal, Fletcher disappears! Gwen taps her braces. Something queer is going on in rock 'n' roll, and it will take some fancy footwork to find Fletcher and make a hit with their new song.

Together again, Gwen, Jill—and Fletcher —solve a musical mystery in another exciting "Something Queer" adventure.

Something Queer in ROCK 'N' ROLL

by Elizabeth Levy

drawn by Mordicai Gerstein

Delacorte Press · New York

To Robie and a lifetime together of good rocking

Published by
Delacorte Press
1 Dag Hammarskjold Plaza
New York, N.Y. 10017

Manufactured in the United States of America

First printing

Library of Congress Cataloging in Publication Data

Levy, Elizabeth.
Something queer in rock 'n' roll.

Summary: Preparing for a rock and roll contest
in which they need a dog's howl over a pizza, the
gang becomes desperate when their dog loses all
interest in pizza.
[1. Mystery and detective stories]   I. Gerstein,
Mordicai, ill.   II. Title.
PZ7.L5827Snl   1987   [E]   86–19772
ISBN 0-385-29547-2

Gwen pounded the piano. Jill flipped her drumstick into the air. Ben's saxophone wailed, and David kept everything steady on the electric bass. Under the piano, Fletcher wagged his tail in time to the music. Gwen and Jill had recently joined a rock 'n' roll band.

"Did you hear about the TV rock contest?" said Gwen when they'd finished their song. "It's for kids under twelve."

"We've got to come up with an original song," said Jill.

"No problem," said Gwen.

But there was a problem.

The group argued over every note. Their music sounded so awful that Fletcher's tail stopped wagging. He put his paws over his ears.

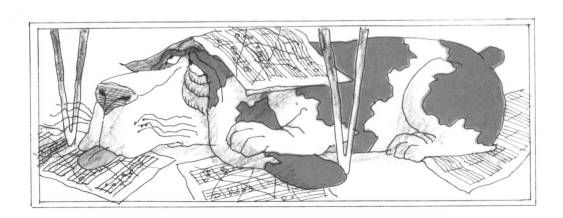

"I'm starved," said Gwen finally. "I can't write another note if we don't eat something."

"Food might be a help," said Jill.

"Let's order pizza," said Ben. "Pizza with pepperoni."

"And extra cheese," said David.

"But no anchovies!" said Gwen.

When the pizza
arrived Fletcher's nose
twitched. He stood up on
his hind legs, plunked his
front paws on the piano
keys, and howled.

Ben and David started
laughing.

"Don't mind him,"
said Jill. "He's hungry all
the time. It's a dog's life."

"That's it!" shouted Gwen. She played chords on the piano and sang, "It's a dog's life."

Suddenly the group wasn't arguing anymore. Within minutes they had written the words and a tune.

"Let's call ourselves Fletcher and the Gang," said Gwen.

"We can wear long ears," said David.

"We can give Fletcher a punk dog collar," said Ben.

"I'm not sure that Fletcher likes punk," said Jill.

"Let's just hope he keeps liking pizza," said Ben. "We need that final howl for the contest."

"Don't worry," said Gwen. "Fletcher will never get tired of pizza."

Fletcher and the Gang went to the TV station for the open auditions.

Hundreds of kids showed up in all sorts of costumes—punk rockers, Madonna look-alikes, young yuppies, and Elvis look-alikes. Nobody else had a dog.

Gwen, Jill, Ben, and David were very nervous. But when Jill held pizza over Fletcher's head, he howled on cue. Then the Gang joined in with a high-pitched "OWW . . . WOOO . . . WOOO . . . WOOOO."

The judges all laughed.

One week later they found out they were finalists. The TV station wanted them at a dress rehearsal on Wednesday.

They decided to practice every day after school.

The next day Jill showed up for rehearsal looking panic-stricken. "Fletcher's missing!" she cried.

"Maybe he found a girlfriend," joked David. "Maybe he's got his first groupie."

"This isn't funny," insisted Gwen.

Gwen tapped her braces.

"Why is she doing that?" demanded Ben and David.

"Because something queer is going on," said Gwen. "Fletcher wouldn't just disappear."

They searched the neighborhood. There was no sign of Fletcher.

Gwen, Jill, Ben, and David put up posters all over town offering a reward. Nobody called.

CLOSE-UP OF POSTER

REWARD!

ANSWERS TO FLETCHER
HOWLS FOR PIZZA
CALL
555-4493

"We're ruined," said Ben. "Without Fletcher's final note, we're nothing."

"I'd give up fame and fortune just to have Fletcher back," said Jill in tears.

Gwen put her arm around Jill. "We have to go to the rehearsal. Fletcher would have wanted us to carry on."

On the night of the rehearsal, Fletcher was still missing. The other finalists had terrific costumes. The Baroos were dressed as mummies.

The Tarantulas had spider suits and wore webbed masks.

The Potatoes had costumes that covered their bodies. Each one was a different kind of potato.

The Teeny-Weeny Boppers wore clown makeup. The lead singer, Willie, was only five; Risa was tiny, but she banged out a mean sound on her toy xylophone.

"We look silly in our Fletcher ears without a dog to howl," grumbled David.

"Where's the dog?" muttered the director. "He was the best thing in your act."

Gwen sighed. "He just wandered off."

"That's rock 'n' roll for you," said the director.

The following day Gwen, Jill, Ben, and David tried to rehearse, but nobody's heart was in it.

Then the phone rang.

"If you want your dog back, go to Durant and Original," said a squeaky high voice.

"Who is this?" Jill demanded.

The caller hung up.

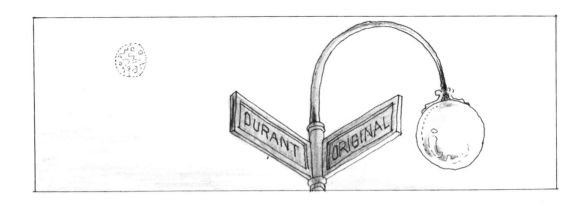

Gwen and Jill ran to the corner of Durant and Original. The street was deserted.

"Look!" Gwen said. She pointed to one of their reward signs for Fletcher taped onto a lamppost. A red arrow pointed to an empty lot. It looked like it had been drawn in blood.

Suddenly they heard a whimper.
"Fletcher!" cried Jill.

Fletcher was standing in a pile of garbage, surrounded by newspapers, empty pizza boxes, and pop bottles.

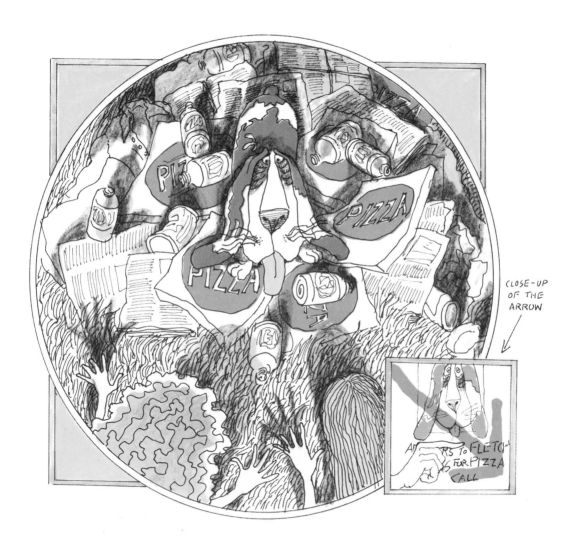

CLOSE-UP OF THE ARROW

Gwen touched the arrow on the lamppost. "It's sticky, maybe it's blood. Is Fletcher cut?"

Jill felt Fletcher all over. "He's a little thin, but I can't find any blood."

They carried Fletcher back to Jill's house.

"Look at this," cried Jill. A piece of light brown felt hung from Fletcher's collar.

"A clue!" exclaimed Gwen.

"What's she, an amateur detective?" asked David.

"Gwen's very good at solving mysteries," said Jill.

"Let's order pizza," said Ben. "Fletcher has to practice his howl."

When the pizza was delivered Fletcher hid under the piano. Jill put a slice under his nose. Fletcher wasn't interested! He wouldn't howl. He hated pizza.

"We're ruined!" exclaimed David.

"Sabotage!" said Gwen with a tap to her braces. "I knew there was something queer about Fletcher's disappearance."

"Maybe he's just tired from his ordeal," said Jill. "We'll try again tomorrow."

On Thursday they ordered pizza. Fletcher hid behind the drums.

They tried on Friday. Fletcher ran out of the room when he smelled pizza.

THURSDAY

FRIDAY

Gwen tapped her braces. "The fiend who force-fed Fletcher cut himself or herself, and wrote the arrow in blood. He or she was also wearing light brown felt. I want to visit each of the other finalists. They all had a motive. Besides, Fletcher might growl if he sees his fiendish feeder."

They took Fletcher to see the Tarantulas, who had added silver studs to their spider costumes.

"Anybody need a Band-Aid?" asked Gwen.

The lead spider gave Gwen a dirty look. "Hey, your dog reminds me of Bruce Springroll," he said.

Fletcher wagged his tail at the fuzzy spider costumes.

"I don't think it's them," whispered Jill.

Next they visited the Potatoes. Mashed Potato was in a foul mood because their lead singer, French Fry, wasn't there.

"He's always late," complained Boiled Potato.

Gwen looked down at Fletcher for any sign of fear.

He had fallen asleep on Baked Potato's drum pedal.

At the Baroos', Fletcher grabbed an end of a mummy wrap and started to pull.

Gwen tapped her braces. Was one of the mummies bandaged to hide a cut?

"Are you all wrapped up as mummies so you don't cut yourself again?" asked Gwen.

"Nobody has a cut," said Ellen, the lead Baroo. Fletcher wagged his tail.

"It's not the Baroos," said Jill. "Let's get out of here before we're all wrapped up."

Willie of Teeny-Weeny Boppers had on a baseball cap. He hugged Fletcher. "Cute doggie," said Willie.

Fletcher licked his face, then he gave tiny Risa a kiss.

"He likes us," said Willie.

"Great," moaned Jill.

Sunday arrived—the day of the live TV show
—and Fletcher still wouldn't howl for pizza. Gwen
was no closer to finding out who had taken him.

"We're gonna bomb," said David.

Gwen, Jill, Ben, and David put on their hound-
dog ears and dog collars.

"Don't worry," said Gwen. "Fletcher and I
won't let you down."

The rest of the group groaned.

On the way to the TV station, they stopped at the pizza parlor. They ordered a pizza.

Gwen tapped her braces. "Has anybody been ordering a shocking number of pizzas?" she asked the owner.

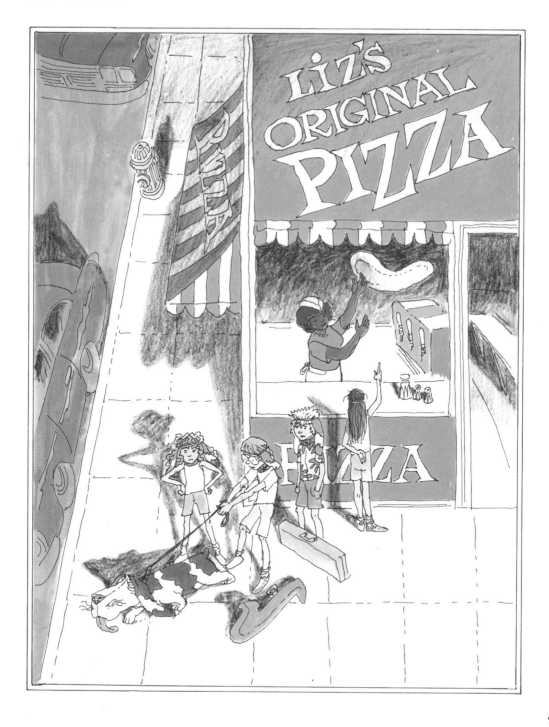

"I'll say," said the owner. "Business has been booming."

"Can you give us the address of your best customer?" asked Gwen. "It's important."

"Well, I don't know what harm it will do." She handed Gwen a slip of paper.

"That's our address," said Jill.

"You've been our best customer, right?" The owner turned to the kid who had been delivering the pizzas to Jill's house.

Fletcher whimpered. He hated pizza!

"Aren't you going to be late again?" the owner asked the kid.

Gwen tapped her braces.

Gwen and Jill took the pizza to the TV station. Gwen looked around for the Potatoes. Boiled was dressed like a red new potato. Baked was wrapped in aluminum foil. French Fry showed up at the last minute in a brown felt costume with cut-out holes for his eyes and mouth.

"I gotta see the poster with the arrow," said Gwen.

Jill dug it out of her knapsack.

Gwen licked the dried-up red arrow.

"Yuk," said Jill.

"It's tomato sauce," said Gwen. "Not blood." Gwen picked up the piece of brown felt she had found on Fletcher's dog collar.

Gwen walked up to the boy dressed as a french fry. Sure enough, there was a patch on the back of his costume.

"Excuse me," said Gwen. "Does this belong to you?" Gwen showed French Fry the piece of brown felt.

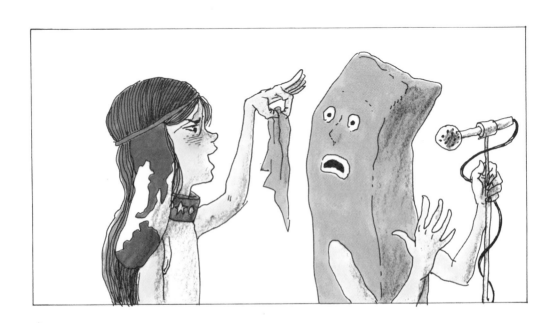

"Where did you find that?" asked French Fry.
"On Fletcher's dog collar!" yelled Jill.
French Fry ran off the stage.

Gwen and Jill chased him, knocking over one of the spiders, unwrapping one of the Baroo mummies. Fletcher flew after the fleeing fiendish French Fry.

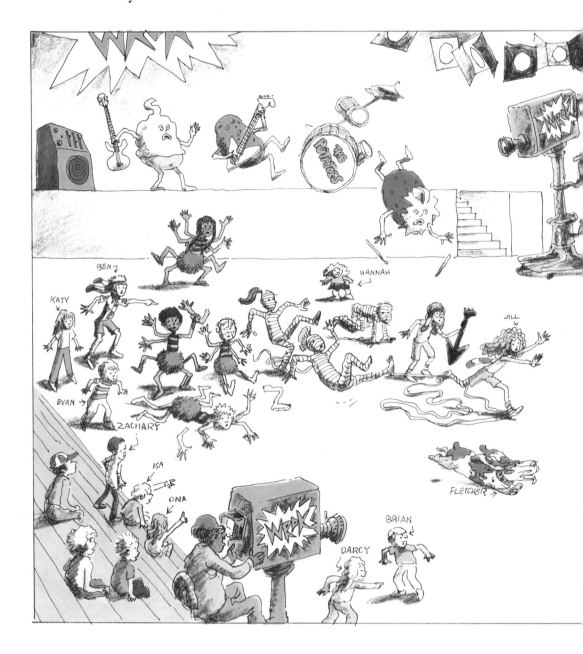

Finally Gwen flipped the pizza at French Fry.
He slipped in the gooey cheese, and fell on the
floor.

Jill tackled him. "I've got the rotten potato," she cried. She had tomato sauce and cheese all over her arms.

"What's going on here?" demanded the director of the TV show.

"Something queer in rock 'n' roll," said Gwen. "That's what's going on!"

French Fry took off the top of his costume. He was the boy who delivered pizza to the house.

"I knew it was you," said Gwen.

"Tell us why you did what you did," said Jill, sitting on French Fry. "Or I'll stuff your mouth with pizza the way you did to Fletcher."

"I knew you got that special sound from that dumb dog," said French Fry. "I watched you rehearse when I delivered pizza. Your dog loves pizza. I hid him in the basement of the pizza parlor and fed him pizzas so he'd get sick of them. But he got so lonely for his owners that he wouldn't eat. I let him go."

"Yeah, but you ruined our song," said Gwen. "Fletcher hates pizza now. He's not hungry all the time."

The director looked frazzled. "French Fry, you're out of the show," he said. "As for the rest of you, we're on live in fifteen minutes."

"Now what?" asked Jill. "Fletcher still hates pizza!"

"Just put on your ears, and pray," said Gwen.

Fletcher and the Gang went onstage, and Fletcher was front and center. But would he howl?

Gwen patted him on the head. "I know you hate pizza, but how about a bite of salami?" she whispered.

Gwen held a tiny piece of salami over Fletcher's head.

Fletcher lifted his head and howled, "OWW . . . WOOO . . . WOOO . . . WOOOO."

"It's a dog's life."

Fletcher and the Gang won the contest paws down.

"Hungry All the Time"

Words by Elizabeth Levy
Music by Ben Harris

A (Chorus)

Hun - gry all the time_____ That's just like a dog's life
Wait - ing for pizza's a crime That's just like a dog's life

That's just like a dog's life_____
That's just like a dog's life_____

B (Verse)   D. S. al **A**

Hold the an - cho - vies   They smell just like old sto - gies
Don't want no sword fish   Don't go well in my dog dish

(Repeat Chorus)
Verse (Repeat Music B)

Want a salami mummy
To pat me on the tummy
Don't want no macaroni
Just pizza and pepperoni

46

(Verse)

I'm___ no___ pus - sy - cat   Not a - fraid of be - ing fat

D. S. al A

I'm not built for chas - ing rats   I'm___ a   dog   who's

(Chorus)

Hungry all the time
That's just like a dog's life
Waiting for pizza's a crime
That's just like a dog's life
OWW..WOOO...WOOO...WOOOO!

ABOUT THE AUTHOR

ELIZABETH LEVY is the author of over thirty-five books for children and young adults, including *Something Queer Is Going On, Something Queer at the Ball Park, Something Queer at the Library, Something Queer on Vacation, Something Queer at the Haunted School,* and *Something Queer at the Lemonade Stand.*

The series has been called "Too much fun to miss" *(Bulletin of the Center for Children's Books),* "a sunny lark" *(Publishers Weekly),* and "sensational" *(Elementary English).*

When not writing, Ms. Levy, who lives in New York City, has been known to pay scalper's prices to see her favorite rock stars. For over thirty years she's been listening to, dancing to, and loving rock 'n' roll.

ABOUT THE ARTIST

MORDICAI GERSTEIN was born in Los Angeles, where he attended the Chouinard Institute of Art. After moving to New York City, he worked for many years designing, directing, and producing animated films for television.

He began doing books for children when he met Elizabeth Levy and they worked on *Something Queer Is Going On,* the first book of the series. In addition to collaborating with Ms. Levy, Mr. Gerstein has also done many books of his own. These include *Arnold of the Ducks, The Room,* and *Tales of Pan.*

Mr. Gerstein lives in a small town in western Massachusetts with his wife, Susan, and their daughter, Risa.